THE HARDY BOYS

BOYS ®

UNDERCOVER BROTHERS™

PAPERCUTZ™

THE HARDY BOYS

#13

UNDERCOVER BROTHERS™

The Deadliest Stunt

SCOTT LOBDELL • Writer

PAULO HENRIQUE MARCONDES • Artist

Based on the series by
FRANKLIN W. DIXON

PAPERCUTZ™

New York

The Deadliest Stunt
SCOTT LOBDELL – Writer
PAULO HENRIQUE MARCONDES — Artist
MARK LERER – Letterer
LAURIE E. SMITH — Colorist
JOHN McCARTHY— Production
JIM SALICRUP — Editor-in-Chief

ISBN 10: 1-59707-102-1 paperback edition
ISBN 13: 978-1-59707-102-4 paperback edition
ISBN 10: 1-59707-103-X hardcover edition
ISBN 13: 978-1-59707-103-1 hardcover edition

10   9   8   7   6   5   4   3   2   1

"THE MAJOR FILM STUDIO THAT IS SPONSORING THIS EVENT--

"-- HAS CREATED AN ALIEN LANDSCAPE TO BEST TEST OUR CONTESTANTS!

"BUT DON'T BE FRIGHTENED! IT ONLY LOOKS LIKE A RIVER OF MOLTEN LAVA!

"CERTAINLY, THIS RUGGED TERRAIN WILL FORCE THESE YOUNG LADIES TO FOCUS AND BRING THEIR A GAME!

TOMORROW IS THE COMPETITION. BUT TONIGHT, WE SHARE A MEAL AS FRIENDS.

YOU ARE ALL CONTESTANTS, YES. BUT YOU'RE FRIENDS FIRST AND FOREMOST.

EVERY STUNT IS PERFORMED WITH EXPERT PRECISION. WITHOUT TRUST--IN EACH OTHER, IN YOUR SUPPORT STAFF--YOU DON'T DARE ATTEMPT ANY STUNT.

I WONDER WHERE DANIELLE IS.

CLAP CLAP

I WAS JUST THINKING THE SAME THING.

IIIIIIIIIIIIIIIEEEEEEEEEE!

IT SOUNDS LIKE ONE OF THE GIRLS!

WE'LL KNOW SOON ENOUGH.

ERRRGH!

I KNOW IT'S ONLY WATER, MOCKED UP TO LOOK LIKE LAVA...

BUT IT LOOKS AUTHENTIC. I AGREE.

IT'S IN KEEPING WITH EVERYTHING ELSE WE'VE SEEN SINCE WE GOT HERE.

FAKE. OR "PUT ON."

STUNTS.

ONE CAMPFIRE LATER...

SO... EVEN THOUGH YOU INSISTED YOU REALLY WERE IN DANGER--

--YOU WERE JUST PRACTICING FOR THE DUEL STUNT PART OF TOMORROW'S EVENT?

IF WE DON'T HAVE AUTHENTICITY, WE HAVE NOTHING.

BUT I GUESS I'M SORRY IF WE SCARED YOU.

G'NIGHT, EVERYONE. I HAVE TO BE UP EARLY TOMORROW.

"SCARED"? I DIDN'T SAY I WAS SCARED.

IN A BIT...

OKAY, I OFFICIALLY DECLARE LINDSAY'S CAR PREPARED FOR VICTORY.

WAIT...!

I'VE GOT TO RECORD YOUR DECLARATION FOR POSTERITY.

SAY IT AGAIN.

● REC

GET OUT OF HERE, GOOFBALL...

THE BOSS HAS A CAR JUMPING COMPETITION TO WIN.

"BOSS." I LIKE THAT SOUND OF THAT, GUYS.

PLAM!

CREAK!

FRANK, LOOK-- THERE WAS NO DRIVER?

THE CAR MUST HAVE BEEN REMOTE CONTROLLED.

LET'S GET OUT OF HERE, NOW. THESE NANOTECH SUITS ARE ONLY GOOD FOR A SHORT TIME.

AS THE COMPETITION CONTINUES INSIDE THE STADIUM, THE AUTHORITIES HAVE COME TO TAKE THE CRIMINAL AWAY...

WHY DIDN'T ANYONE TELL US ALL THE DETAILS OF THIS CASE BEFORE HAND, DAD?

A.T.A.C. HAS TO TRAIN NEW AGENTS IF WE INTEND TO CONTINUE FIGHTING CRIME ON BEHALF OF TEENS ACROSS AMERICA.

WE WERE AFRAID IF THE SUPPORT TEAM KNEW ABOUT JEREMY, THEY WOULD BE TOO INCLINED TO HELP.

AND POSSIBLY UNDERMINE THE WHOLE EXERCISE.

I WAS WONDERING WHY NONE OF THE EVIDENCE POINTED TO THE THREE "SUSPECTS."

YOU WERE KEEPING US *INVOLVED* IN CASE LINDSAY AND JEREMY NEEDED HELP...

...BUT NOT CLOSE ENOUGH TO STEP ON THEIR TOES.

EPILOGUE: "HERE'S TO USING YOUR HEAD..."

Don't miss THE HARDY BOYS #14, "Haley Danelle's Best Eight"

NANCY DREW

A NEW GRAPHIC NOVEL EVERY 3 MONTHS!

#1 "The Demon of River Heights"
ISBN 1-59707-000-9 pb.

#2 "Writ In Stone" ISBN 1-59707-002-5 pb.

#3 "The Haunted Dollhouse"
ISBN 1-59707-008-4 pb.

#4 "The Girl Who Wasn't There"
ISBN 1-59707-012-2 pb.

#5 "The Fake Heir" ISBN 1-59707-024-6 pb.

#6 "Mr. Cheeters Is Missing"
ISBN 1-59707-030-0 pb.

#7 "The Charmed Bracelet"
ISBN 1-59707-036-X pb.

#8 "Global Warning" ISBN 1-59707-051-3 pb.

#9 "Ghost in the Machinery"
ISBN 1-59707-058-0 pb.

#10 "The Disoriented Express"
ISBN 1-59707-066-1 pb.

#11 "Monkey Wrench Blues"
ISBN 1-59707-076-9 pb.

NEW #12 "Dress Reversal"
ISBN 1-59707-086-6 pb.

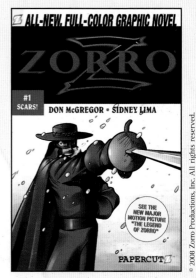

ON SALE NOW!

All: Pocket sized, 96-112pp., full color, $7.95
Also available in hardcover! $12.95 each.

Nancy Drew
Boxed Set #1-4
384 pages of color comics!
ISBN 1-59707-038-6

Nancy Drew
Boxed Set #5-8
432 pages of color comics!
$29.95 ISBN 1-59707-074-4

ZORRO

1. "Scars!" ISBN 1-59707-016-5
2. "Drownings!" ISBN 1-59707-018-1
3. "Vultures!" ISBN 1-59707-020-3
4. "Spies in Space" ISBN 1-59707-055-6
ch: 5x7½, 96pp., full color paperback: $7.95
so available in hardcover! $12.95 each.

At your store or order at Papercutz, 40 Exchange Place, Ste. 1308,
New York NY 10005, 1-800-886-1223

PAPERCUTZ

WATCH OUT FOR PAPERCUT𝘡™

If this is your very first Papercutz graphic novel, then allow me, Jim Salicrup, your humble and lovable Editor-in-Chief, to welcome you to the Papercutz Backpages where we check out what's happening in the ever-expanding Papercutz Universe! If you're a long-time Papercutz fan, then welcome back, friend!

Things really have been popping at Papercutz! In the last few editions of the Backpages we've announced new titles such as TALES FROM THE CRYPT, CLASSICS ILLUSTRATED, and CLASSICS ILLUSTRATED DELUXE. Well, guess what? The tradition continues, and we're announcing yet another addition to our line-up of blockbuster titles. So, what is our latest and greatest title? We'll give you just one hint -- the stars of the next Papercutz graphic novel series just happen to be the biggest, most exciting line of constructible action figures ever created! That's right -- BIONICLE is coming! Check out the power-packed preview pages ahead!

Before I run out of room, let me say that we're always interested in what you think! Are there characters, TV shows, movies, books, videogames, you-name-it, that you'd like to see Papercutz turn into graphic novels? Don't be shy, let's us know! You can contact me at salicrup@papercutz.com or Jim Salicrup, PAPERCUTZ, 40 Exchange Place, Ste. 1308, New York, NY 10005 and let us know how we're doing. After all, we want you to be as excited about Papercutz as we are!

Thanks,

Jim

EDITOR-IN-CHIEF

Caricature drawn by Steve Brodner at the MoCCA Art Fest.

TWO DOZEN TEEN DETECTIVE GRAPHIC NOVELS NOW IN PRINT!

You know, while it's exciting to be adding so many new titles, we don't want anyone to think we've forgotten any of our previous Papercutz publications! For example, can you believe there are now two dozen all-new, full-color graphic novels starring America's favorite teen sleuths?! Let's check out what's happening in the 12th volume of NANCY DREW...

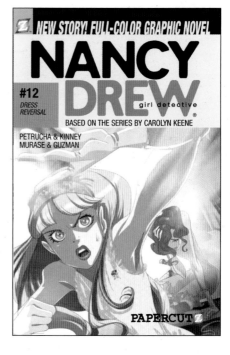

Writers Stefan Petrucha and Sarah Kinney and artists Sho Murase and Carlos Jose Guzman present Nancy's latest case, "Dress Reversal." After showing up at River Height's social event of the year, in the identical dress as the party's hostess, Deirdre Shannon, things get worse for Nancy when she's suddenly kidnapped! That leaves Bess, George, and Ned to solve the mystery of the missing Girl Detective.

That's all in NANCY DREW #12 "Dress Reversal," on sale sale at bookstores everywhere and online booksellers.

Behold. . .

At the start of the new millennium, a new line of toys from LEGO made their dramatic debut. Originally released in six color-coded canisters, each containing a constructible, fully-poseable, articulated character, BIONICLE was an instant hit!

The BIONICLE figures were incredibly intriguing. With their exotic names hinting at a complex history, fans were curious to discover more about these captivating characters. Even now, over six years later, there are still many unanswered questions surrounding every facet of the ever-expanding BIONICLE universe.

A comicbook, written by leading BIONICLE expert and author of most of the BIONICLE novels Greg Farshtey, was created by DC Comics and given away to members of the BIONICLE fan club. The action-packed comics revealed much about these mysterious biomechanical (part biological, part mechanical) beings and the world they inhabited. A world filled with many races, most prominent being the Matoran. A world once protected millennia ago by a Great Spirit known as Mata Nui, who has fallen asleep. A world that has begun to decay as its inhabitants must defend themselves from the evil forces of Makuta.

The first story arc of the comics called "The BIONICLE Chronicles," begins when six heroic beings known as Toa arrive on a tropical-like island which is also named Mata Nui. The Toa may just be the saviors the people of Mata Nui need, if they can avoid fighting with themselves, not to mention the Bohrok and the Rahkshise early comics are incredibly hard-to-find, and many new BIONICLE fans have never seen these all-important early chapters in this epic science fantasy. But soon, those comics will be collected as the first two volumes in the Papercutz series of BIONICLE graphic novels.

These early comics are incredibly hard-to-find, and many new BIONICLE fans have never seen these all-important early chapters in this epic science fantasy. But soon, those comics will be collected as the first two volumes in the Papercutz series of BIONICLE graphic novels.

In the following pages, enjoy a special preview of BIONICLE graphic novel #1...

AND THE *DARKNESS CANNOT STAND* BEFORE ME.

BIONICLE 1:

GREG FARSHTEY·WRITER
CARLOS D'ANDA·PENCILLER
RICHARD BENNETT·INKER
ALEX SINCLAIR·COLORIST

I HAVE SLEPT FOR SO *LONG*. MY *DREAMS* HAVE BEEN *DARK* ONES.

BUT NOW I AM *AWAKENED*.

NOW THE SCATTERED ELEMENTS OF MY BEING ARE REJOINED.

NOW I AM *WHOLE*.

DON'T MISS BIONICLE GRAPHIC NOVEL # 1 "RISE OF THE TOA NUVA"

CLASSICS
Illustrated

Featuring Stories by the World's Greatest Authors

Returns in two new series from Papercutz!

   The original, best-selling series of comics adaptations of the world's greatest literature, CLASSICS ILLUSTRATED, returns in two new formats--the original, featuring abridged adaptations of classic novels, and CLASSICS ILLUSTRATED DELUXE, featuring longer, more expansive adaptations-from graphic novel publisher Papercutz. "We're very proud to say that Papercutz has received such an enthusiastic reception from librarians and school teachers for its NANCY DREW and HARDY BOYS graphic novels as well as THE LIFE OF POPE JOHN PAUL II...*IN COMICS!*, that it only seemed logical for us to bring back the original CLASSICS ILLUSTRATED comicbook series beloved by parents, educators, and librarians," explained Papercutz Publisher, Terry Nantier. "We can't thank the enlightened librarians and teachers who have supported Papercutz enough. And we're thrilled that they're so excited about CLASSICS ILLUSTRATED."

Upcoming titles include The Invisible Man, Tales from the Brothers Grimm, and Robinson Crusoe.

FULL-COLOR GRAPHIC
NOVEL ADAPTATION

CLASSICS
Illustrated
Deluxe

THE WIND
IN THE
WILLOWS

By Kenneth Grahame

Adapted by
Michel Plessix

PAPERCUT*Z*

A Short History of
CLASSICS ILLUSTRATED...

William B. Jones Jr. is the author of Classics Illustrated: A Cultural History, which offers a comprehensive overview of the original comic-book series and the writers, artists, editors, and publishers behind-the-scenes. With Mr. Jones Jr.'s kind permission, here's a very short overview of the history of CLASSICS ILLUSTRATED adapted from his 2005 essay on Albert Kanter.

CLASSICS ILLUSTRATED was the creation of Albert Lewis Kanter, a visionary publisher, who from 1941 to 1971, introduced young readers worldwide to the realms of literature, history, folklore, mythology, and science in over 200 titles in such comicbook series as CLASSICS ILLUSTRATED and CLASSICS ILLUSTRATED JUNIOR. Kanter, inspired by the success of the first comicbooks published in the early 30s and late 40s, believed he could use the same medium to introduce young readers to the world of great literature. CLASSIC COMICS (later changed to CLASSICS ILLUSTRATED in 1947) was launched in 1941, and soon the comicbook adaptations of Shakespeare, Stevenson, Twain, Verne, and other authors, were being used in schools and endorsed by educators.

CLASSICS ILLUSTRATED was translated and distributed in countries such as Canada, Great Britain, the Netherlands, Greece, Brazil, Mexico, and Australia. The genial publisher was hailed abroad as "Papa Kassiker." By the beginning of the 1960s, CLASSICS ILLUSTRATED was the largest childrens publication in the world. The original CLASSICS ILLUSTRATED series adapted into comics 169 titles; among these were Frankenstein, 20,000 Leagues Under the Sea, Treasure Island, Julius Caesar, and Faust.

Albert L. Kanter died, March 17, 1973, leaving behind a rich legacy for the millions of readers whose imaginations were awakened by CLASSICS ILLUSTRATED.

CLASSICS ILLUSTRATED was re-launched in 1990 in graphic novel/book form by the Berkley Publishing Group and First Publishing, Inc. featuring all-new adaptations by such top graphic novelists as Rick Geary, Bill Sienkiewicz, Kyle Baker, Gahan Wilson, and others. "First had the right idea, they just came out about 15 years too soon. Now bookstores are ready for graphic novels such as these," Jim explains. Many of these excellent adaptations have been acquired by Papercutz and will make up the new series of CLASSICS ILLUSTRATED titles.

The first volume of the new CLASSICS ILLUSTRATED series presents graphic novelist Rick Geary's adaptation of "Great Expectations" by Charles Dickens, the bittersweet tale of one boy's adolescence, and of the choices he makes to shape his destiny. Into an engrossing mystery, Dickens weaves a heartfelt inquiry into morals and virtues-as the orphan Pip, the convict Magwitch, the beautiful Estella, the bitter Miss Havisham, the goodhearted Biddy, the kind Joe and other memorable characters entwine in a battle of human nature. Rick Geary's delightful illustrations capture the newfound awe and frustrations of young Pip as he comes of age, and begins to understand the opportunities that life presents.